Dear Parents

As we all know, from an early age, the information our children learn about religion will later influence their beliefs, attitudes, and behaviors in later years.
This series tells about the birth, infancy, and childhood of Prophet Muhammad (peace and blessings be upon him), with stories and drawings that will appeal to our children and help them to understand.
We hope and believe that you and your children will enjoy this series and find the stories not only entertaining, but informative as well.

2

THE NIGHT OF WONDERS

It was a warm evening in Mecca. The sky was full of bright stars that looked close enough to reach out and touch. Nearly all of the gazelles were grazing near Mecca, and chatting while they ate. The oldest of the gazelles looked at the sky, and full of wonder. He said: "How bright the stars seem tonight." At that moment the youngest gazelle noticed a new star being born. She jumped up and down in excitement. "Look, everyone, look!" she cried "A new star is being born. The other gazelles saw the newly born star, and they all said: "How beautifully Allah has created that star!" They then glanced at one another. The beautiful peaceful night made them feel full of love and wonder.

Suddenly, a wave of excitement came over the oldest gazelle.

"Hey, everyone! I have a feeling that something very important is going to happen tonight. Listen, can you hear anything? Everybody has gone quiet. It's like they are waiting for someone. The sky is full of brilliant and sparkling stars. We have all just seen a new star being born. Let's try to find out what's going on. What do you think - should we look around and see what's up?"

The gazelles thought that this sounded like a good idea, and agreed that everyone should go off in a different direction to explore. They arranged to meet by the big date-palm tree at sunrise to tell each other about what they had seen.

Her heart beating fast, the youngest gazelle trotted off toward the town. Before she had gone far, she spied a house different from the others. The entire town was in darkness, but this house was brightly lit. It was the house of Amina. The little gazelle wondered why all the lamps were burning here. She started to wander around the house, curious to see if she could find out what was happening. She was eager to discover why this house was lit while all the other houses were dark and quiet. Just then a beautiful scent of roses floated past her on the breeze. This heavenly scent was coming from Amina's house. Oh, Allah, what a glorious smell! All at once the house was surrounded by a dazzling light; the garden was flooded with a heavenly glow. Suddenly, the youngest gazelle realized that while she had been exploring she hadn't noticed the time; the Sun would be rising soon. Time had just flown past while she had been watching Amina's house.

Just then, two women came
out of the house. It was clear
that they were happy, but
they also seemed surprised by
something. As they talked,
one woman said to the other:
"I have never seen such a
beautiful baby before.
They have called him
Muhammad."
Her friend could only nod in
agreement she was so
overwhelmed by what she
had seen in the house. The
youngest gazelle began to
understand; this was where
the Baby Muhammad was
born - the baby for whom
the whole world had been
waiting. His arrival had
put an end to the silence
all around.

The birds had started to sing, the leaves of the trees had started to rustle and whisper among themselves. Weaving its way through the trees, the breeze celebrated the birth of this baby. All the living creatures showed their joy in different ways. The youngest gazelle ran happily to the date palm tree to meet her friends. She settled down to wait for them, but it was very difficult for her to keep still; she could hardly wait to start to tell them her story!

12

As the Sun rose, the other gazelles arrived at the tree. Breathlessly, the youngest gazelle started to explain what she had seen. "Hey, everyone! Tonight a baby was born. When he was born, the scent of roses filled the air and everywhere was lit by a glowing light. I heard that the baby is very beautiful and that he smiles at everything around him. They named him Muhammad." All the other gazelles listened with great attention to what she said. She had described everything so well that all the gazelles became just as excited as she was; they felt like they too had been in Amina's garden. After listening to what the little one had to say, the oldest gazelle understood everything.

With tears of joy falling from his eyes, he began to speak. When he spoke, all the other gazelles went quiet and listened with great respect to what he had to say:

"This is great news everyone, great news. The baby that our little friend has told us about is the Baby of Light. He is the last prophet, Muhammad, and all the people are waiting for him. That bright star was born for him. The roses gave off a more beautiful scent than usual because of him. Everything fell quiet for him. How lucky we are to live at such a time," the oldest gazelle said.

All the gazelles leaped with joy. The gazelles, the trees, the flowers . . . in short all of creation, was full of joy. It was as if a great holiday had been pronounced over all the Earth because our beloved Prophet Muhammad (peace and blessings be upon him) had come into the world.